Ann Bryant is a children's author and a music educationalist. She has written around 120 books in these two fields and, as well as writing, gives school author talks and music education workshops both in the UK and abroad. To find out more about Ann visit her website: www.annbryant.co.uk

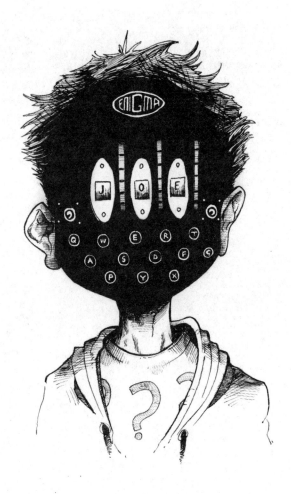

Breaker

Ann Bryant

I'm Joe ... don't.

A Catalogue record for this book is available
from the British Library.
ISBN: 9780995488557

Printed and bound by CPI Group (UK) Ltd, Croydon, CRO 4YY

The paper and board used in this book are natural recyclable products
made from wood grown in sustainable forests. The manufacturing
processes conform to the environmental regulations
of the country of origin.

Caboodle Books Ltd
Riversdale, 8 Rivock Avenue
Steeton, BD20 6SA, UK
www.authorsabroad.com

DAILY STATUS

1.1

My First Daily Status

Hello! I am writing my first Daily Status. I was wondering how you thought up the idea of the Daily Status being like a kind of diary, Mr. Clark. I mean I know you're a teacher, and teachers have to make things up for English, but it was still quite clever thinking of it. I'm looking forward to when the author comes at the end of term and some people read bits of their diaries out loud. You said we're going to do a status every school day till the end of term and I've worked out that if this first status is called 1.1 the very last one will be 8.5. I like that way of numbering the entries. It's a kind of code.

So here's a bit about me. My name is Joe Barnes. I live at 3 Beech Court with my mum. Her name is Annie Barnes. Our house is a Bed and Breakfast house. That means that sometimes people stay with us. It's Mum's job. My best friends are Noah and Olly. My hobby is cycling and doing stuff on my bike like wheelies.

That's my first Daily Status entry. I'm not sure it's any good. Noah wrote loads. Olly didn't. But Olly's got an excuse. Everyone knows he's not much good at reading and writing and stuff. Anyway Mr.

Clark said it didn't matter how short our entries were. The trouble is I don't know what to write. I've already made it up about my hobby being cycling and I definitely can't do wheelies. I've no idea what to write tomorrow. Or the next day. Or the next. Or the thirty six after that. I'm going to have to make more stuff up because there is absolutely nothing more to say about me that's not private.

I said I lived with my mum but that's all I can say about my family. It's the littlest family in the world. I've never had a dad and I don't have brothers or sisters. The only way I can see my family getting any bigger is if Mum gets a boyfriend and has a baby, and that would be gross. Mum hasn't got any brothers or sisters either so I don't have any cousins. Noah's got four cousins who live in New Zealand, lucky thing. He says his family is going to visit them soon. I don't have anyone to visit outside England. I don't even know anyone outside England. My grandma died when I was four. Apparently I've got a grandfather but I've never met him. Mum said she wouldn't want to inflict his presence on her worst enemy let alone her son.

I asked Mr. Clark if it was okay to talk about friends and stuff, and he said, "Absolutely! You can write about whatever takes your fancy." At least that's given me an idea for tomorrow's Daily Status.

1.2

The New Girl

Today I am writing about the new girl in our class. She's got red hair. Lots of people call her names. She doesn't care. Here's one of the names she gets called, only it's in code – Potato Bottom. (Can you work it out, Mr. Clark? The second word is an opposite and the first word is another vegetable.) She's passed her Bikeability test. We haven't got Bikeability at our school, otherwise I'd do it too.

And now for the truth. I really really like the new girl. But nobody knows that. Nobody. Not Noah. Not Olly. Definitely not the new girl. She's called Berry T O Smith. (That's how she writes her name on her schoolbooks anyway.) I heard Mr. Clark say, "Berry, Tess, Olivia. Those three names go brilliantly together!" And in my head I agreed. No one else was listening because they were getting their packed lunches out, but it got me thinking about my own name – Joseph Barnes. Only two names. I wish I'd got three. Berry has got dark ginger hair and a few freckles. Her eyes are green and they really stand out in her face. When people call her rude things, she looks at them like they're poo on a shoe or a maggot or mould. And somehow that makes people like her more, but they pretend they don't. I can tell they do, though, because I've got detective eyes.

There are other popular girls in the class like Dina Ray. She's got black hair and she says things like '*You* guys!' and 'Tell me about it!' and 'No pressure then!' And I think that's what makes her popular. Not with me though. I'd rather have Berry Smith any day. She comes to school on her bike. I'm going to practise cycling until I can ride no hands. I've started practising in the car park near us. I have to do it really early or really late when there are hardly any cars around. It'll be great when I'm good at it and Berry looks at me with big respect.

1.3

Breaking Codes

*My main hobby is code breaking. (I'm glad you noticed that, Mr. Clark!) It's a bigger hobby than cycling. I also like code **making**. Here is one I made up today. Can you get it, Mr. Clark? Here's your clue:*

You have to swap one of the letters in the first word with one of the letters in the second word, then you have to swap one of the letters in the third word with one of the letters in the fourth word.

Coke breading if sun.

When Mr. Clark looked at my second Daily Status he said it was very good but he'd been looking forward to reading more about my cycling. He asked where I'd been on my most recent bike ride and his eyebrows shot right up when I said Havely Hill. It was just the first place that came into my head because I know really good cyclists go up there for a challenge. I was expecting him to congratulate me but I was dreading it in case he told the whole class because then Olly and Noah would know I'd made it up. But luckily he just said, "Oh, right. Jolly good." Then he changed the subject and said, "Thank you for bringing to my notice that some people

11

are being unkind and calling Berry names. Name-calling is definitely not allowed in this school and I will be dealing with the culprits." Then he said it was sensitive of me to put the name in code, and asked if code making was another hobby of mine.

It was like a rocket went off inside me because I realized it was kind of true. "Yes, it *is!*" I said. "And also code breaking. Codes in general are a big interest of mine." I was exaggerating like mad but the main excitement was because this was going to solve my Daily Status problems. I could keep writing code after code right till the end of term. Result! I gave Mr. Clark a massive grin and he nodded and smiled a quick smile. "Excellent stuff. There you go then, Joe. Sorted."

1.4

Bed And Breakfast

Our Bed and Breakfast is like an overflow for Fernleigh Guest House. When they get extra bookings they phone us. They got one yesterday so we had someone called Ari staying with us. He is American and he's really nice. Here's the name of our Bed and Breakfast. I've written it in code. Can you work it out, Mr. Clark?

The clue is this: The first word is the name of a precious stone and the second word is what you call a little house.

Ddnomai Cegatto

I'm getting really good at codes now. In my Daily Status today the letters are in reverse order except for the first one. I tried it out on Mum and she said she didn't have time for code breaking when she was trying to cook breakfast, but that was just an excuse. The truth is she couldn't crack it.

Mum's always busy in the mornings. Well she's busy all the time actually. I sometimes wish she wouldn't do Bed and Breakfast, except that it earns us money. I don't usually like having complete strangers in our house. But I like Ari. He's travelling around England for eight weeks. Actually he should be called Hairy not Ari. There's so much hair on his chest it comes right over the top button of his shirt. His arms are hairy too.

Mum went bright red when I called him 'Hairy' by mistake. She started hissing at me to say sorry, and the hissing reminded me of a snake. Then Ari started laughing, which reminded me of a hyena. It was over breakfast when it happened. Ari had just come back from his early morning jog. He said he was going to take a shower. I asked him where he was taking it *to*. He didn't get the joke. Mum did, but she didn't appreciate it because as soon as Ari had gone out she said, "Joe, for goodness sake! It's embarrassing with you around!" And I said, "With me around *what*?" And Mum said, "Oh, cut it out!" So I got the scissors.

I wish Berry Smith could have been a fly on the wall. Then she'd have seen me being cool and clever. I also wish I could write all that in my Daily Status but 1: it's too long and 2: I might have felt cool when it happened but it wouldn't look cool written down. At least now I've got two things to write about in my Daily Status: 1) codes 2) the people who stay at our Bed and Breakfast. None of them will be as nice as Ari though. He says he'll send us a postcard occasionally when he's left us to carry on his tour of England.

1.5

My Grandfather

My grandfather died yesterday night. Mum told me at breakfast time. We didn't have anyone staying because Ari's gone. It was just me and Mum. I was eating my cereal at the time. It's that new brand called Snip-Snaps. I don't like the actual cereal very much, but every packet has got a Snip-Snap person in it and I want to collect the whole set. I always hope the Bed and Breakfast people will choose Snip-Snaps for breakfast so we can get through it faster. Mum's going to my grandfather's funeral in about a week. She's really sad. And I will miss him too.

Mum's not at all sad about her father dying. She's not seen him for fifteen years. But it's got me thinking about Grandma Mel. That was my grandfather's wife, only they were divorced. She died when I was four. I can remember that clearly. I knew she was ill but I didn't know she was going to die right then. I remember I was telling her about the storm outside, and she didn't reply. And I remember Mum with tears rolling down to her chin, saying, "She can't hear you, Joe. I'm afraid she's died."

People told me Grandma Mel had left her body behind and gone to heaven because her heart wasn't working. I asked if she'd got a new body in heaven and Mum said she thought she had. I don't like it when grown-ups *think* things but don't actually *know* them. Everyone seemed sure about heaven though. They said it was higher than the clouds, higher than where the planes go, higher than the stars.

I went into the back garden and tried shouting out to Grandma Mel but I must have been too loud because Mum said, "All right, that's enough now, Joe. I don't think the neighbours are going to be very impressed with you breaking the sound barrier." I said I'd stop when Grandma replied. Mum said, "When people are dead they can't reply." Then she added, "But Grandma will have definitely heard, so you can stop now." I said, "Do you *think* she will have heard me, or do you actually *know*?" Mum said she knew for sure. But her voice didn't *sound* all that sure, so I went out and did one more big shout to tell Grandma Mel not to worry that she couldn't reply.

I thought I saw some sadness in Mum's eyes when she was staring across the kitchen this morning, but it couldn't have been because, like I said, she's not sad.

2.1

Head Lice

For a joke I pretended I'd got nits but I haven't. No way. I've never had nits. (You can examine my head if you want, Mr. Clark! That'll prove it.) No, I just said it for fun because I'm quite interested in nits. Did you know they can crawl 23 centimetres in a minute and are the second most catchable thing after a cold? This is code for how long they can live without a meal of blood from someone's scalp.

The clue is: Write out the alphabet and put numbers under every letter from 1 to 26 so A is 1 and B is 2. Then change the letters to numbers and the numbers to letters and you will crack the code!

DH   8, 15, 21, 18, 19

Yesterday was a tough day at school. No one wanted to come near me. This is why…

There's a boy in our class called Croppo. That's because he's got cropped hair. I can't remember when he got it cropped and I don't remember how it used to look before. All I know is that everyone's a bit scared of him. The thing is, I don't think anyone was scared of him before he got his hair cropped.

So I thought maybe I ought to get my hair cropped too. Not so people'd be scared of me. Just because I think Berry Smith might notice me with cropped hair. On the other hand it might make me look stupid. So I decided to ask Mum's advice. This is how the conversation went.

ME: Ever thought about changing your hair to make yourself a bit cooler, Mum?

MUM: (kind of panicky) Do you think my hair's too long for my age?

ME: No, do you think mine is?

MUM: (laughing a bit) No, you weirdo, Joe!

That didn't get me very far. But then I had the coolest idea. Why not just ask Berry. So I made sure I was taking my plate up at the end of lunch at exactly the same time as her, then I said, "Hey, Berry. I was thinking of getting my hair cropped. What do you think?" And she stopped scraping her plate off and looked at me like I was a rare specimen of nature, for about ten seconds. Then she said, "Look, Joe, the good thing about you is that you don't care about your image, so don't shatter my illusions OK?"

When I worked out what she was talking about, I felt stupid, so I put on a bit of a sneer and tried to look cool, and said, "No, you've got it wrong. See, I don't want to cut it because of my image." And she said, "Why then?" And I said the first thing that came into my head. "Cos... I've got nits."

And she broke into this massive grin starting with her eyes. So, like I said, today was a tough day at school once Berry had spread the news.

2.2

Top Secret Business Idea

*Me and Olly and Noah are setting up a business. It was Noah's idea because he wants to be an aren'trapanneur when he grows up. (I meant entrepreneur, Mr. Clark. Just looked it up. In the thesaurus it says another word is speculator.) I looked that up in the dictionary and it says that if you speculate, you invest in stocks or property. Well maybe Noah will do that one day because he's got a big brain. But right now he's got this top- secret business idea. (I can't even tell **you**, Mister Clark!)*

Olly, Noah and I are setting up a pizza delivery business. I don't really see how it's going to work, but Noah gets lots of ideas about making money the whole time and this is just another one. He says Olly's got to be the chef. Olly says there's a small problem - he doesn't know how to make pizzas. I think that's a big problem, but Noah says it'll be a piece of cake because you can easily find out how to make the bottoms, and then you put whatever you want on the top. Noah saves money all the time. He calls it investing it. He's going to buy ingredients for the pizzas with some of it then Olly's got to find a time when his mum's out so he can make loads and store them in the freezer.

I'm the delivery boy. I've not been riding my bike in the car park much lately so I'm a bit nervous about carrying pizzas and wobbling. I asked Mum for a big basket to go on the front but I didn't tell her what it was for, and she told me that people had baskets on their bikes in the old days. So now I don't want one because I don't want to look old fashioned. Then I thought I'd carry the pizzas in a rucksack on my back. But Noah said the toppings would slide off because of the pizzas being on their sides.

So I've come up with this great idea. I'm going to carry them on my head. I once saw a film with Indian ladies carrying jugs of water on their heads, and pizzas must be much easier. I'll practise walking with a book first, then I'll try it on my bike. Like Noah says, it'll be a piece of cake! In fact, a piece of pizza! (Wish Berry Smith could have heard me saying that.)

2.3

Detective Work

*Knowing that Noah wants to be an entrepreneur when he grows up has got me thinking what **I** want to be. Well, I reckon I'd make a good private detective because I can crack codes and because I'm good at noticing things. I like the thought of following clues and following people and checking up on them and solving crimes.*

I wish I wasn't so good at following clues actually, then I wouldn't have noticed all the new things Mum's suddenly got. New trousers. New posh top. New shoes. Two new pairs of earrings. New belt. I first got suspicious when I saw her wearing the new top and trousers at the same time because Mum only ever buys one thing at once. But then I saw she was wearing new earrings – well first I heard them rattling whenever she turned her head. So then I started looking out for other signs of spending money and I saw the new belt and the new shoes and the other new pair of earrings. I asked Mum where she got the stuff from and she said Debenhams. She gave a sort of secretive smile. I've no idea why. I asked her if she'd got a new job to be able to afford all that stuff and she just smiled and shook her head.

2.4

Dogs

Yesterday when our neighbour was walking home, a dog started following her. She didn't know what breed it was but she said it was quite little. Personally I like big dogs better than little ones, and my favourite would be a Great Dane. Mum prefers little dogs. Anyway that got me thinking about dogs so I made up some codes for you Mr. Clark. These are all well-known breeds of dog, and I've given you clues, don't worry!

- ***Xlsxtixn*** *(x = **a** certain letter)*
- ***Eagle going after a buzzing insect*** *(There are only two main types of buzzing insect and it's not a wasp. Just put eagle after the other sort.)*
- ***Little Swede*** *(You should get this one easily once you've read my Daily Status!)*
- ***Cowcat*** *(Think of a male cow to get you started.)*
- ***Fighter*** *(Think of someone who does a sport that involves fighting)*

So yesterday I met a dog. It wasn't a Great Dane unfortunately. It was a like a little dirty ball of fluff that only came up to my ankles and you couldn't see its eyes for hair. I think it was in competition with Ari, except that the hair on its chest was matted and dirty. (Do you call it a 'chest' on a dog?)

Anyway, it followed me all the way home. I kept on turning round and saying, "Shoo, Scruffball." But it didn't.

I was dreading Croppo or Berry seeing it trotting after me. So it was a big relief to get home I can tell you.

Then about two hours later Mum suddenly said, "Joe, there's a dog sitting outside our gate." And when I went to the door Scruffball wriggled under the gate and came trotting up wagging its tail like it was my mate coming to see if I wanted to hang out. I told it to shoo in my gruffest growl but Mum said, "Don't be mean. Poor little thing." And the nutter dog suddenly bolted straight past me into the living room.

I really thought Mum'd go mad then, because it was making the carpet dirty, but all she said was, "Let's give it a bath. It's the least we can do." I tell you, if we bath Scruffball, it's going to look like a baby's toy, all white and fluffy. I've got to get rid of it before anyone (e.g. Croppo/Berry/Noah) thinks we own it. (I don't mind about Olly. He won't judge me. But he'll tell the others, because he spills secrets like some people spill drinks at school dinners.)

2.5

Bletchley Park

Bletchley Park is a really interesting place. (Good suggestion about looking it up, Mr. Clark!) This is what I found out.

During the Second World War there was a top-secret operation going on at Bletchley Park. It was just a big old country house where a group of friends went to stay one weekend and everyone thought they were ordinary people having a nice holiday. But they weren't. They were MI6 code-breakers! They were trying to crack the enemies' codes to work out their secret messages so the army would know what their plans were.

We might not have won the second world war if it hadn't been for the people working at Bletchley Park. They had amazing machines to help work out the codes, and also the world's first computer that was called Colossus. The most difficult code they had to decipher was a German one called Enigma. During the war the code for Enigma changed at least once a day so there were 159 million million million possible solutions!

I'm really pleased Mr. Clark told me to look up Bletchley Park. It sounds amazing. I want to go there. I might ask Mum if we can. By the way, we've abandoned the pizza idea. Olly told Noah he couldn't make them, thank goodness, so I didn't have to admit to Noah that I couldn't deliver them (for about 159 million million million different reasons that Mum came up with!) And another thing, we haven't had any Bed and Breakfast people since Ari, so thank goodness I've got codes to write about!

3.1

My Book

I've got another kind of hobby now. Writing. I'm writing a book but most of the work is in my head. It's all about codes and code breaking and clever detectives from history. I don't want to say any more about it in case anyone takes my idea (e.g. you, Mr. Clark!) You never know when you're going to get a sudden burst of inspiration. It could be in the middle of a bike ride for example. In fact that's actually what happened to me the other day.

So I got talking to Berry Smith and told her I was going to deliver pizzas on my head on my bike, but Noah had decided against the Pizza Delivery business because Olly couldn't make them. I should have guessed she'd find that highly hilarious. But when she'd finished laughing her head off she suddenly said, "Want to come on a bike ride at the weekend?" I couldn't believe my ears and I said, "Yes," really quickly before she could change her mind.

Trouble was I didn't want to go on a bike ride or she'd see how rubbish I was, so when I got to her house I said, "Let's just go on a walk." She gave me the maggot look then, and told me I could borrow her big brother's 21-gear bike, while she rode her own 3-gear one.

I started talking about everything I could think of so she'd lose interest in the bike ride. For example, there was a violin case in her living room and she said she used to play violin at her old school and was hoping to start lessons again soon. I quickly said I liked violin too and that my mum was looking for a teacher. Her eyes lit up like she was really pleased we had something in common. She said if I started lessons we could play duets. Then she suddenly said, "Come on. Let's get on with the bike ride!"

It went just as badly as I thought. She got ahead in no time. This is the first excuse I made up for why I couldn't keep up. "Sorry, Berry, I'm not used to posh bikes."

Big mistake. She offered to swap. So I was left puffing and panting and feeling like a fossilized dinosaur on her 3-gear bike.

When the gap between us had widened to about half a kilometre, she looked back. It looked like she was laughing, so I got off the bike and sat on the grass verge. After a while she cycled back to me and asked me what I was doing.

I'd already planned what to say. My idea had come from Olly in a way. You see, he's just started Karate to help with his co-ordination. I told Berry I'd got a big Martial Arts competition coming up and the teacher said I wasn't really supposed to cycle because it uses all the wrong muscles.

Berry looked at me like I was growing mould out of my ears, and that was when a much better excuse popped into my head. "OK this is the real reason," I said, trying to look a bit mysterious. "The thing is, I'm writing a book," I told her, "and I have to concentrate really hard whenever inspiration hits me, and it's just hit me now so you may as well carry on without me."

She rolled her eyes, got back on her bike and pedaled off. She hasn't spoken to me or looked at me since. If only Mr. Clark would ask for volunteers to read out their Daily Status, right now. Then Berry would believe it's true I'm writing a book, and she might start talking to me again. Otherwise I'll have to wait until the author comes at the end of term before I can read it out. And that's ages.

3.2

Straw To Gold

The title of this Daily Status is something to do with the play we're doing at school. I've made up a code for the actual title of the play, Mr. Clark.

It's 1 word with 4 syllables in it.

1st syllable: **A word for an animal's bottom**
2nd syllable: **Spanish for 'the'**
3rd syllable: **Things you walk on to make yourself really tall**
4th syllable: **A word I'd never heard of before that means relations.** *(I looked it up in my Thesaurus, Mr. Clark!)*

Yesterday we had the first rehearsal. Everyone in the whole school is in the play. The little ones are doing the bit about turning the straw into gold. I don't know how they're going to do it.

Berry has got the main part. She has the best voice in the school. It's amazing.

I know it's only a fairy tale but I like the idea of straw turning to gold. I keep getting this picture of dirty brown straw turning lighter and lighter, then going yellow and then gleaming like gold only still in very thin strands all bunched up like noodles.

Berry sings loudest out of all the girls in our class. She doesn't care when people stare at her. Except I stared at her once and she gave me the maggot look back.

3.3

More About Bletchley Park

You wanted to know something else about Bletchley Park, Mr. Clark, so here goes! As more and more people joined Bletchley Park, some of the workers moved into wooden huts dotted about on the lawns. It was all so top-secret that the huts were only called by numbers.

The codes they had to break at Bletchley Park were way harder than any of the codes I've made up. Loads of women who were from the Women's Royal Naval Service (called WRENS!) helped speed up the code breaking by using machines called Bombes. (Not bombs!)

They wanted people who were really clever with numbers to break the codes, and they found that mathematicians from Cambridge and Oxford universities were the best. They chose Bletchley Park to be the code breaking headquarters because the railway line used to run between the two universities and stop at Bletchley on the way.

By the way, we got a postcard from Ari yesterday. He's in Cambridge.

Mum has just announced that she's not doing Bed and Breakfast any more. I think it might be because of Scruffball. The mad dog likes sitting in the middle of the stairs, and that's kind of dangerous. I mean it wouldn't look good if one of the guests tripped over him, toppled down and knocked themselves out, would it?

Mum did everything to try to trace Scruffballs's owner, but nothing worked. When he had a bath he came out looking like a ball of white fluff, just like I predicted. So now Mum's calling him Fluffeta Sue. It's a girl but I'm pretending it's a boy and I'm calling it Enigma Scruffball.

3.4

The Code Club

Olly and Noah and I have formed a code club. We had our first meeting at Olly's the other day and I've realized that people use codes the whole time. Here's an example: Olly's little sister, Dora, has got this soft toy dog called Jack that she carries around with her absolutely everywhere, and Olly's mum is trying to get Dora to give Jack up because he's smelly and tatty.

Anyway, yesterday Olly's mum was just about to take Dora to something called 'Stay and Play' club. And I heard her say to Olly's dad, "Don't mention the canine. He's not featuring on this outing." I didn't know what she was on about till Olly whispered to me, "Canine means dog. Dora's not allowed to take Jack, you see."

The trouble was, Olly's whisper was not a whisper, so Dora heard every word. And the main word must have got her thinking because she suddenly piped up, "Where's my Jack?" And Olly's mum gave Olly a look as if to say, 'Thanks very much!' in a sarcastic way.

Here's another example of a kind of code that's used every day, but this one's written down on a price tag. £79.99. That's code for £80.00. The shopkeepers put £79.99 to make people believe they're paying much less money that £80.00, when in fact it's only a penny less.

OK so I'm seriously worried now. Mum is scaring me. She's got another new top and a new scarf. There's no way she can afford all this stuff, especially now she's not even doing Bed and Breakfast. So if she can't afford it, then she must be a...

3.5

About My Grandfather

You asked if I wanted to write a bit about my grandfather, Mr. Clark. So that's what I'm writing about today.

I called my grandfather Granddad. He was tall and quite thin and a very good sportsman – especially at cycling. Mum says that's where I get my cycling skills from. He cycled from London to Paris once to raise money for charity. He used to play all sorts of games with me, but he lived quite a long way away so we didn't see him all that often. He was a great man. Mum keeps listening to this piece of music they played at his funeral. She says it's very famous and it's got violins in it. I really like it too now.

I can't concentrate on anything at school because I can't stop thinking about Mum being a thief all the time. And if I'm not thinking about that I'm thinking about my grandfather. It was true what I wrote in my daily status about him being a good cyclist and riding all the way from London to Paris, and it was true about the piece of music they played at his funeral. The rest was made up. I feel bad telling lies about him to Mr. Clark but I didn't know what else to say. Mum still doesn't want to talk about her father. I've managed to squeeze a few facts out of her, though.

- He divorced Grandma Mel a long time ago when Mum was only five.
- He was fifty at the time, which was a lot older than Grandma Mel.
- Mum still visited her dad when she was a girl.
- As she got older she didn't want to see him any more because she was cross with him for leaving her and Grandma Mel.
- She thinks the very last time she ever saw him she was about twenty.
- She definitely isn't sad.
- He married someone else when he left Mum and Grandma Mel.
- Mum saw the new wife at the funeral.
- Mum *definitely* doesn't like the new wife. She absolutely refuses to tell me anything about her.

I hate being an only child with no other relations but Mum.

4.1

The Admissions Box

At school in assembly our Head Teacher talked about making wrong things right. She's put an Admissions Box in the hall. She said that if you've done something wrong and you wish you could make it right, you can write it down and put it in the box. She also said that only the teachers will see it and they won't tell you off but they might want to talk to you about it. It's just to make you feel better if you're feeling guilty about something.

I wonder if Mum feels guilty. I'm really worried that she'll get caught stealing one of these days if I don't do something about it. So when the Head Teacher invented the Admissions Box it got me thinking about making wrong things right, and I made a plan. I carried it out on Saturday.

Mum was gardening and I told her I was going round to Olly's. But first I secretly found a big bag and carefully put all Mum's new clothes and earrings and stuff in it. Then I went to the bus stop and caught the bus to Debenhams.

Jewellery in Debenhams is quite near the entrance on the ground floor, so that's where I started. I spent ages looking at earrings, pretending I was choosing a pair when actually I was looking round without moving my head. Just my eyes flicked from side to side. Checking. When I was certain no one was watching I took Mum's earrings out of the bag and put them back next to an identical pair. It felt weird doing reverse shoplifting.

It was when I was feeling around in the bag for the other pair that someone spoke from right behind me. "What's going on here then? Helping ourselves to a spot of jewellery are we?" I jumped about a mile into the air then turned to see a man in a suit. He was giving me a suspicious look. "Actually I'm putting the earrings *back*," I said in my politest voice. He did something that might have been a cough or might have been a snigger. "Now I've heard everything!" Then he looked in my bag and said, "Come on, sunshine. You've got some explaining to do."

That was when I saw Berry Smith and a lady that must have been her mum, out of the corner of my eye. Berry gave me the longest look ever as I walked off with the man. I know I went red because I could feel my cheeks burning. If she tells everyone at school, my life will be terrible.

4.2

Buried Names

Can you find the name that is buried in all of these words, Mr. Clark?

Robot
Problem
Probe
Robe
Strobe

I didn't feel like writing anything more in my Daily Status so it came out really short. You see, this is what happened at Debenhams.

The man who carted me away to explain stuff was like a store detective. He took me to the store manager. The store manager phoned Mum. She showed up. I thought she'd have to pay a massive fine or get taken to court. But it turns out she's been going out with the store manager without saying a word about it to me, and he's been buying her presents. Mum went red when she explained it to me. Then I went red. Then the manager went red. Then Mum introduced me to him. (His name's Rob. I hate that name.) Then they both laughed and Rob stroked Mum's arm and I felt this big anger boiling up inside me, and told Mum she was stupid and pathetic. Then I walked off.

(So far Berry hasn't said anything about seeing me in Debenhams to anyone in the class. At least no one's said a word to me about it.)

4.3

What To Do If You Find A Stray Dog

- *Keep it in your house while you wait for the owner to show up*
- *Contact the police*
- *Put an advert in the paper*
- *Contact the council*
- *Go to 'Pets Located' online*

You might want to know why I'm writing about this, Mr. Clark. It's because of that neighbour I mentioned. The dog that followed her is still at her house so I looked up what she could do.

Facts about Scruffball:
- He likes being carried
- He refuses to go on walks. He just sits there. If you put a lead on him, he plays dead and you finish up dragging him along, so you have to stop.
- He likes it in Mum's handbag.
- He prefers human food to dog food.
- He gets scared if you sneeze. (Mum's friend Mel came round the other day. She's got hay fever and every time she sneezed, Scruffball yelped and fell over trying to get away quick.)
- He farts a lot.

4.4

Morse Code

Morse code is brilliant. (I forgot that was a type of code, Mr. Clark!) Every letter of the alphabet is represented with a combination of dots, dashes, or dots and *dashes. The most famous Morse Code is SOS. That's a distress signal that means 'help!' and you can do it with a mixture of short and long sounds (for the dots and dashes) or with a flashlight or a torch or a mirror (with short and long flashes) or on a computer or even just with blinks. It looks like this:*

. . . _ _ _ . . .   (which is dot dot dot dash dash dash dot dot dot.)

The navy, the army and the air force all use Morse code. Once there was a radio operator on an old ship and he had a stroke and couldn't speak or write but he let his doctor know what he wanted to say by blinking! It's amazing that you can send messages to people just by blinking.

In the Rumpelstiltskin rehearsal Mr. Clark wanted a volunteer from the boys to sing a solo. He kept looking at me because I'd been singing loudly in all the songs. I only did that to be like Berry. But singing a solo? No, that was not going to happen. Ever. I'd be too

embarrassed. So I looked down to make sure I wouldn't get picked. When I dared to look up again Mr. Clark was looking right at me. "Joe?" he said hopefully. "You'd be great."

I noticed Berry's eyes were wide with waiting to hear what I'd say. It felt good to know that she was looking at me with big interest and not big disgust. Maybe she'd even start talking to me again if I sang a solo. Then Croppo smirked and said, "Go on Joe. Your country needs you!" And the whole class laughed. Even Mr. Clark laughed but he stopped quickly and said, "No, seriously, you'd be really good, Joe." "Yes," said Croppo, making out he was being sincere, "your mummy would be so proud of you."

Croppo made me sick. "That's enough commentary from you, Lewis," Mr. Clark said sternly to Croppo. (Lewis is his actual name.) "Yes be quiet, Croppo," said Dina Ray. But she gave him a look like she didn't really want him to be quiet. I shook my head.

"Is that a no, Joe?" asked Mr. Clark. I nodded. "Oh well, we'll just have to do without a solo then," he said with a sigh.

So the rehearsal went on and I bet everyone else forgot all about what had just happened. But I didn't. I couldn't. Not with Berry's eyes flashing me maggot looks the whole time. Maybe it was her own secret code. Maybe she was blinking a message like the radio operator on that ship. If it *was* Morse code, I'm glad I didn't understand it. I don't think I would have liked whatever she was trying to say.

4.5

Jobs

If it was wartime I'd definitely want to be a code breaker. I've been researching other jobs like that and I could be a crossword compiler because that's all about making codes in a way. Apart from being an author, of course, the only other job I'd like is being a detective. Dogs make the best detectives. You can train them to sniff things out like drugs and money and firearms.

I'm still cross about Mum having a secret boyfriend. She goes and on about Rob but I refuse to even say his name. The only good thing about it is that she's sucking up to me quite a bit these days. That's how come we wound up at the airport yesterday after school. (Mum sucking up. She had to drive for over an hour.) I told her I wanted to see sniffer dogs at work as I'm thinking of being a sniffer dog handler when I grow up. That's not actually true. I just wanted to try out an experiment. Mum called me a dingbat and said it was ridiculous going to an airport just to look at sniffer dogs. But she still took me.

Then she got really into it because she spotted a golden Labrador approaching us. "Ooh, isn't he lovely, Joe!" she said.

What Mum didn't know was that I'd got explosives down my pants wrapped in a tissue. OK, not exactly explosives, but a party

popper. I've read that party poppers have got a tiny amount of gunpowder in them. So that's kind of explosives, right? You see, Noah and I had this argument about sniffer dogs. I said they could detect gunpowder even if it's only one grain and it's inside a piece of fluff in someone's belly button with loads of clothes on top of it. Noah said that was rubbish. I wanted to prove him wrong, only I couldn't fit the party popper in my belly button so that's why I put it down my pants.

So this is what happened. The dog pulled the handler urgently in our direction, and I thought, no it can't be. It can't be! And half of me was happy because it looked like this was the proof I needed, but the other half was panicking about what was going to happen next.

The dog started sniffing the top of my trousers, barking its head off. I had my tomato head on and Mum was speaking out of the corner of her mouth in her hissy voice with big gaps between every word. "***What   is   going   on   Joe?***"

So I was right about sniffer dogs. It's true, they *can* detect the most miniscule amount of explosives hidden under about a million layers of clothes. This means that finding the party popper in my pants must have been the easiest work that dog had done for ages. Lucky old dog got a reward. Me, I got arrested. Well…kind of.

The good thing about saying I'd been arrested was that Noah was impressed. He spread it round the whole class, then everyone was impressed. Everyone except Croppo.

I hate how Croppo can do that. He said it was pathetic boasting about an arrest. And because he's like the king of the class, everyone started sucking up to him, saying things like, "What kind of loser gets arrested?" In the end I told the truth to stop all the comments. "It wasn't an arrest. Just a telling-off." I thought that would make everyone be nice to me again but Croppo went all sneary and said it was pathetic boasting about a telling-off. I said I wasn't boasting, but no one was listening by then.

The only person who didn't say a word was Berry Smith. I think it might have been better if she'd said something. The way she never speaks to me or looks at me is horrible. It's like I don't exist.

5.1

Something From The Monopoly Board!

We went to see an old friend of Mum's at the weekend.
The journey took ages. We parked the car at the station
and went on the train to London. Then we went on the
tube to Liverpool Street Station. That's one of the stations
in Monopoly. It was funny seeing it in real life. Then we
went to Norwich, which took ages and ages. That's where
Mum's friend lives. She's got a long thin garden covered
in brambles. She says she likes it like that. Mum says she's
eccentric. (That means slightly strange.) She's nice though.
And VERY clever.

Oh, and we got another postcard from Ari on
Saturday. From York.

When Mum said we were going to see an old friend of hers, I said
I didn't want to go. That was when Mum told me it wasn't exactly
an old friend. Her exact words were, "Actually it's my stepmother.
Your step-grandmother, Joe. The woman your grandfather lived
with after he left Grandma Mel. She's called Rosalind, OK?"

I tell you, a very old moth could have knocked me over in one
flutter of its papery wings when Mum said that. I didn't know what
to say, so I said the first thing that came into my head. "I thought
you didn't like her." Mum just grunted which wasn't an answer. So

when we were on the train, I said it again, and made it sound like a question. "I thought you didn't like your stepmother?" But Mum grunted again, so I tried a different question. "Is she rich?"

This was Mum's reply. "No idea. Haven't seen her for years. Apart from at the funeral. Didn't like it when my father left us and went to live with *her*. Never asked for a step-mother. Didn't see the point. Or the need."

I'd never heard Mum talking in sentences with words missed out before, and I didn't like it. Also, something was confusing me. "So…er…why are we going to see her now all of a sudden?" Mum shrugged and said it was because Rob thought it was a good idea. I stopped the conversation after that. How come Rob makes decisions about our family? It's nothing to do with him.

These are the good things about my step-grandmother:

1. She doesn't ask loads of questions.
2. She doesn't like cooking so we just ate things like crisps and biscuits and olives, and bread dipped in lovely tasting sauces, all day long, and never had a proper meal with a knife and fork.
3. She's got a whole book of puzzles. Hard ones. She spent ages helping me do them.
4. She says that next time we visit her we can see Norwich Cathedral. I thought that might be quite boring but she says there's a maze there and she wants to see if I can find the way to the centre.

These are the bad things about her:

1. Her house has two spare rooms so she might invite us to stay over one day and I'm not sure if I want to.
2. She said she hadn't been called Rosalind for years and we should call her Roxy. I don't mind saying Roxy when I'm talking about her to Mum, but it was embarrassing actually *calling* her Roxy. I noticed Mum didn't call her anything. So then neither did I.

3. Roxy talked about Mum's dad quite a bit and I could tell
    Mum didn't like that because she looked down all the time.
    It turns out Mum's dad had MS. That stands for Multiple
    Sclerosis. It's an illness. In the end he couldn't move or see
    or speak properly. That doesn't happen to everyone who
    has MS but it happened to Mum's dad. Roxy had tears in
    her eyes when she talked about him. Then Mum did too.

So it's **4:3** in the good v bad competition. Afterwards Mum asked
me if I wanted to see Roxy again. I said, "It'd be good to see the
maze at Norwich Cathedral." And Mum rolled her eyes. (The look
on her face said, *Well THAT won't be happening.*)

5.2

Anyone Want A Dog?

If you want to keep a stray dog, you can adopt it but you have to tell the council, and if the real owner turns up, even if it's after years, you have to give it back. Our neighbour has now adopted that stray dog I wrote about. But she's changed her mind and doesn't actually want to keep it any more. Do you want it, Mr. Clark? (It's little and quite cute.) Or if you don't want it yourself perhaps you could ask round the whole class if anyone wants it. It's free and I could easily bring it into school. Our neighbour said that would be fine with her.

When Mum started to get excited about keeping Enigma Scruffball I started panicking. I told her I wouldn't walk anywhere with her if she had a dog farting in her handbag. People might not see the dog and think it was me. Also I still think Noah would find it one big joke that we'd got such a silly looking dog and I wouldn't want him spreading it round the class. The trouble is, it's hard making up excuses for why we can't have Code Club meetings at my house. It was OK at first but I'm having to be really inventive now. The latest excuse I made up was that we're getting the whole house repainted and every room is a mess and Mum says no visitors for a fortnight. Mr. Clark says he can't really ask if anyone wants a dog until he hears from Mum.

Once a week in assembly we have 'thinking time' where it's totally silent for individual thoughts about anything you want. Some people pray during that time. I didn't used to. But I do now. This is my prayer. *Please let Mum decide to give Enigma Scruffball away or let his owner turn up and collect him.* If I say that sentence six times slowly, it fills the whole thinking time.

It hasn't worked though. An owner hasn't turned up and Mum says we're definitely keeping him. She doesn't like the name Fluffeta Sue any more and she definitely doesn't like Enigma Scruffball. She's decided to call him Cashew, because cashew nuts are a kind of white colour and nuts are little. I thought that was a silly idea but Mum liked it.

Trouble is, 'Cashew' sounds like 'A-tchoo!' So the nutter dog runs away whenever you call its name.

5.3

Birthdays

It was Mum's birthday yesterday. I got her something from the charity shop that she really wanted. I managed to get it home from the shop and smuggle it into the house without Mum seeing. She was really happy with it. Can you break the code, Mr. Clark? Here's your clue: Get a mirror!

Won thgir otni gnikool era uoy tahw

This year I gave mum a mirror so she can check her eye stuff. Sometimes when we're out, like in a shop or a café Mum kind of hisses at me. "Joe, look at my face. Have I got any black under my eyes?" (She means make-up.) And I usually say yes, just to see how fast she moves, trying to find a mirror. Then she comes back and says, "Joe, there's no black under my eyes. Why did you say there was?" And I just grin at her but she doesn't grin back.

Anyway, one time when she asked me, I said no. (I was feeling kind that day.) Mum said, "Are you sure, Joe?' three times. The last time it was in her snake voice. *"Are you sure Joe?"* Then she got up from her chair in a big stress and went to check anyway. "See?" I said, when she got back. And she just glared. So that's why I got her a mirror.

When she opened it, I explained it was to keep in her bag when she went out, so she could do her own checking. And she said, "Joe, I can't take this around in my handbag. It's massive!" I knew that really but I was hoping she'd got a bag that was big enough because I didn't know where to buy little mirrors. Then Mum cracked up and said, "Joe, you're so funny. But never mind, I'll put it on the wall then I can ask it the million pound question *Mirror, mirror on the wall, who is the fairest of them all?* I grinned at that because I got it. It's what the wicked stepmother says in Snow White.

So then I did my own joke back. It was much funnier. "Mirror mirror in my bag, who's that big fat ugly hag?"

For some reason Mum didn't appreciate it. (Maybe I'll try it on Berry. It might be just the thing to get her noticing me again.)

5.4

Guess The Name Of The Show

Here's a new type of code for you, Mr. Clark. This is the name of a really good show that I went to see with my mum. It was awesome. Some people might think it's for girls but there were lots of boys and men in the audience. This is the title.

<><><>R<><><><><>iv<><><><>,<<<><><><>
<><><><><><><><><><><><><><><><>e
r<><><><><>>>><><><><><><><><><><><><>
<d<><><><><><><><>>>>>>>><a<><><><><n
><><><><><><><><><><><<><<><><><><><><
><><><><><><>>>>ce.

We went to see a dance show for Mum's birthday. I didn't tell anyone because it was embarrassing. There were other boys in the audience but they looked different from me. Smarter, for one thing. And they'd all got sisters too. I felt stupid being a boy out with his mum. And I didn't want anyone to think Rob was my dad either, so I sat on the other side of Mum in the theatre and only said 14 words to Rob in the whole evening.

> *Okay* (when he asked me how I was.)
> *Thanks* (when Mum hissed at me to say thank you.)

No thanks (when he asked if I wanted a programme.)
No thanks (when he asked if I wanted a drink.)
Okay (when he asked if I wanted an ice cream.)
Yes please (when Mum hissed at me that I didn't deserve
an ice cream if I was going to be so surly all evening.)
Fine (when he asked me how school was going.)
It was okay (when he asked me if I'd enjoyed the show.)
Bye (when he said 'Bye Joe. Good to see you.')

The show turned out to be awesome. Loads of men and women
Irish dancing, beating rhythms on the floor with their hard clicky
shoes and kicking and bouncing and making patterns with the
loudest music ever. I wish I could see it again.

The English Language

*This is something I got from Mum's friend – the one who
lives in Norwich and is VERY clever - English is weird!
This poem will show you why it's so weird, Mr. Clark.
Me and Mum's friend made it up together.*

Weird *rhymes with* **beard**
Beard *is a weird* **word**
Because you don't spell it **beird**.
And **word** *is also* **whirred.**
Which rhymes with **bird**.
Bird *rhymes with* **turd**.
A **bird** *sits on a* **bough.**
Bough *rhymes with* **how**.
How *do you* **do**?
Do *rhymes with* **poo**.
And **through**.
And **grew**.
So it's **true**.
English is **weird.**

Like I said, there's only me, Noah and Olly in the Code Club. But
the other day Noah said we ought to open it up for other people to

join. I said "Like who?" And he said, "Dunno. Maybe someone like… Berry Smith or someone?"

He was trying to sound casual but I knew at that moment, with my detective eyes on Noah, that he really liked Berry. And that made my stomach go into the tightest knot on earth. Then he said we ought to take a vote on it.

Noah's vote was yes. My vote was no and Olly said he was abseiling.

I laughed and explained to Olly that abseiling means climbing down a rock face or a high building with a rope round your waist. Noah said that Olly meant he was choosing not to vote, like in the Houses of Parliament. So then I thought I must have got the wrong word because Noah is never wrong about stuff.

When I got home I asked Mum if MPs did abseiling in the Houses of Parliament. She laughed for so long I thought she must have been remembering a whole heap of funny jokes. And when she finally stopped breaking into giggle-splutters about three hours later, I asked her what the real word was.

So the word is abstaining, right. I can't wait to tell Noah Know-All. I'm going to really rub it in. Abseiling in the Houses of Parliament!

6.1

Nutty Jokes

I got these jokes from that friend of Mum's who lives in Norwich. Her name is Roxy. It's a bit of a funny name, I know.

Roxy said "Give me a topic, Joe. Any topic, and I'll give you a joke about it."

We were eating peanuts at the time because she likes snacks, so so I said, Peanuts!" And this is what she came up with!

Q: What do you call a peanut in a spacesuit?
A: An astronut!

Q: Did you hear the joke about the peanut butter?
A: I'm not telling you. You might spread it!
Q: What did the peanut say to the elephant?
A: Nothing. Peanuts can't talk.

I asked Mum when we were going to see Roxy again. She just shrugged and didn't answer. So I asked her again. She said she wasn't sure if she wanted to see her again because she still couldn't forgive her for taking her father away from her mother. But then she sighed and said, "I suppose it takes two to Tango." I think she meant it wasn't just Roxy's fault that her dad left her mum. It was her dad's fault too. Then Mum said, "…and after all, Roxy did look after my father through his MS." I could see tears in Mum's eyes then, and I felt sorry for her.

To make her feel better I got the nuts out. She loves nuts. But then she got cross with herself because some of the nuts were so hard she wasn't strong enough to make the nutcrackers work. Neither was I.

So I secretly got a hammer. Unfortunately I forgot to move the nuts off the big plate they were on. That was messy, I can tell you.

Mum went ballistic. She asked me who in their right mind would think of cracking a nut on top of a china plate. I said, "Someone who comes from China?" thinking that might make her smile, but she stayed mad. So I tried again. "Someone who's nuts?" And she turned round so she wasn't facing me, but I saw her face in the mirror and she was actually smiling. Phew!

6.2

Elgar

*I'm getting interested in more kinds of music now. Mum
listens to the same piece of music over and over again at
home. I don't know what it's called but it says Best of
Elgar on the CD cover. It's got violins in it. I'd quite like
to play the violin. Elgar's a composer. I've worked out
that if you change the letters of ELGAR around you can
make three more words – LARGE, GLARE, LAGER.
They're called anagrams. Clever eh, Mr. Clark?*

Mum is obsessed with the piece of music by Elgar. I asked her why
she likes it so much and she said it was played at her dad's funeral.
One day I saw she was crying and I asked her why, and she said it
was because she felt guilty that she hadn't seen him before he died.
She said to me, "Whatever you do, Joe, don't fall out with someone
you were once close to. You'll only regret it."

That got me thinking about Berry. Was I once close to her? I
think I was. But now she doesn't want to be friends any more. I'm
wondering why. Is it because she knew I was making it up about
writing a book when we were on that bike ride? Or is it because she
thinks I'm a thief? Or is it because I didn't volunteer to sing a solo
in the school play? Or is it because I said I got arrested at the airport?
Or is just a mixture of all of those things? It's weird with Berry. Like

you have to pass a test to be her friend. And so far I've failed every time. I think I've got to be more honest. She seems to really like honesty, even if it stops you being cool.

Noah asked her if she wanted to join our Code Club. She said, "Who's in it?" Noah said, "Me, Olly and Joe." Berry said, "No thanks."

6.3

Mnemonics

*I have been Skype messaging Mum's friend from Norwich, who is called Roxy, by the way. She's really interested in words. We've been talking about words with silent letters at the beginning like **g**nome and **k**nife and **p**sychiatrist. She asked me if I knew what a **m**nemonic is. You might not know this Mr. Clark, but it's something to help you remember stuff. Like if you can't remember the colours of the rainbow, here is a mnemonic to give you the first letter of all the colours in the same order as they appear in the rainbow.*

> *Richard - **R**ed*
> *Of – **O**range*
> *York – **Y**ellow*
> *Gave – **G**reen*
> *Battle – **B**lue*
> *In – **I**ndigo (which is like a dark purple colour)*
> *Vain – **V**iolet*

I don't really like that mnemonic so I've invented my own one. Roxy thinks it's really good.

Really Old Yak Gave Birth In Vicarage

It's strange how you can be told something when you're little and you keep believing it when you're older. It's only now I'm older that I realize that Mum made up stuff about Grandma Mel dying because I was little at the time. All the same I wanted to check up on that. So today I asked her if it was true what she'd said back then. "It's true for me, Joe," she said.

I've thought about that loads and decided it's true for me too. The other thing she told me was that there was a rainbow in the sky when I was talking to Grandma Mel and she thought that was a sign that Grandma had heard me. I like thinking about that. I've decided that rainbows are always signs of good things.

6.4

After School Activities

Mr. Clark was talking to our class about all the different activities that take place at school. Then we had to say what we'd like to do. I'm not really interested in doing anything because I've got enough with the code club and my bike and the book I'm writing.

As soon as I heard the list of different activities you could do after school I felt really excited because one of them was violin. When Mr. Clark said that one, Croppo started laughing in a loud mocking voice and Mr. Clark calmly said to him, "What a strange reaction, Lewis."

Croppo always answers back and he said, "It's a weird thing to do – try to make sounds by dragging a bow across some strings." He was looking round as he said that and quite a few people joined in laughing or sniggering. Mr. Clark replied, "Well it would be weird if that was what playing the violin involved. But it's not. It involves acquiring a technique through practice in order to make the most amazing music."

While Croppo tipped his head on one side and gave Mr. Clark one of his Croppo looks, I started thinking about that piece that Mum keeps listening to by Elgar. And something happened inside me like a bird fluttering up to my throat and I couldn't wait for my turn. I was going to pick violin for my activity.

But it was Berry before me. "Which activity appeals to you, Berry?" said Mr. Clark. Berry stuck her chin up and looked directly at Croppo. "Violin," she said in her clear voice. Croppo smirked but he didn't say anything. Then it was my turn and I felt a wave of nervousness come over me. A few seconds before I'd been all ready to say violin because I'd forgotten that Berry had lessons at her old school, but now that she'd said it, I wasn't so sure any more. Croppo would definitely laugh and that would make everyone laugh. I made a mistake and glanced at Berry. Her eyes were like glinting steel with magnets in them, stopping me from looking away.

"Joe, what about you?" said Mr. Clark. Berry seemed to be daring me to say violin. My heart started banging so loudly I thought the people nearby would be able to hear it. And suddenly I was speaking and these were the words that were coming out of my mouth. "I don't think I'll do any activity actually."

The magnets seemed to lose their power after that, and Berry's gaze dropped to the floor. So did mine. I felt like a pile of camel dung.

6.5

Transport

Find the hidden form of transport, Mr. Clark. Here's your clue:

> *You have to work out all the forms of transport, then find the extra letter in each one, then put all those extra letters together to make the hidden one.*

Buss Tracin Ploane Shoip Cart Beike Varn

After school Noah and I went round to Olly's for a meeting of the Code Club. After a while we ran out of things to talk about. But Olly's mum said it was OK for us three to take Dora out on her scooter as long as we kept a proper eye on her. I thought it might be a bit boring and slow but it turns out Dora is the fastest nearly-three-year-old on a scooter *ever*! As we got nearer and nearer to the town centre she got further and further away from us. We were yelling out, "Dora, stop!" But she couldn't hear us. Olly asked me and Noah to catch her up but Noah said he didn't feel like running so I did it on my own.

I ran like the wind and when I caught up with Dora she was smiling up at a woman who was wearing a look of big time annoyance. "Is this young lady with you?" barked the woman. I gulped but I didn't have to say anything because Dora was doing the talking. "Aksherly I'm a girl not a young lady," she said. The woman was still looking at me. "She's just bumped into me," she said a bit crossly. Dora looked at the lady as though she felt sorry for her, and said, "You wasn't looking where you was going, was you." The lady's eyes nearly popped out of her head. "Are you going to stand there and let her take that tone?" she snapped. Dora did a more dramatic sigh. "I didn't take the tone," she said patiently. I thought the woman was about to blow a fuse. Her whole face was wobbling with crossness. "Scooters are dangerous things on pavements," she said. I opened my mouth to reply but Dora beat me to it again. "Scooters aren't allowed on the road, you see," she explained gently. "So I'm afraid I *have* to ride on the payment." The woman stood there spluttering for a bit then stuck her chin in the air and marched off.

After a while Olly and Noah showed up. "Everything... all right?" asked Olly, sounding kind of hesitant. "Yes I sorted it out," I replied, keeping my cool. But Dora had her hands on her hips and a challenging look in her eyes. "Aksherly *I* sorted it out," she said. "And it's naughty to tell lies, Joe," she added, wagging her finger at me. Olly and Noah fell about laughing. And I couldn't help joining in. And that's when Rob suddenly appeared.

Rob acted liked coming across us three was the most exciting thing that had ever happened to him. He looked from me to Olly to Noah and back to me like he was waiting to be introduced. In my flattest voice I said, "This is Olly. This is Noah. This is Rob." And Rob said a really bright squeaky hello to Olly and Noah while they just stared. Then he whizzed off, mumbling about being a bit late.

After he'd gone Noah asked me who he was. I said he was just someone Mum knew. I didn't get asked any more questions, thank goodness.

7.1

Norwich Cathedral

On Saturday Roxy took me and Mum to Norwich Cathedral. It was very grand and the people looking round it were totally silent. The maze was awesome. Roxy says it's actually a labyrinth. It's like a massive circle carved into the ground with little parts of circles, that are called arcs, carved inside the big circle. Some of the arcs are dead ends.

You have to start walking at the outside and try to walk all the way to the centre along the little pathways without coming to a dead end. There's only one possible route you can take that doesn't have any dead ends. Roxy said that other mazes are built with hedges and in fields of corn and even indoors with mirrors. She knows a lot about puzzles and mazes.

Mum and I looked round the market while Roxy went to some ordinary shops. (She said she'd been to the market loads of times before and she had some things she needed to buy from the shops.) It turned out to be a kind of trick!

I wanted to try to solve the puzzle of the maze by starting in the centre and finding out the route that way, but Roxy said that was cheating. She said I had to use concentration and memory then I'd be able to do it. And she was right, because I did it in the end!

I'm glad Roxy's my step-grandmother. I wish Mum liked her more though. Roxy invited us to stay over Saturday night and spend Sunday with her. Mum said we didn't have any overnight things. Roxy said, "I thought you might say that, so I took the liberty of buying a few things when you were looking round the market." Then she produced two toothbrushes, a tube of toothpaste, some face cream stuff for Mum and two pairs of jamas, one for me, one for Mum.

I was laughing because Roxy had been so clever, but Mum looked cross. She said, "You shouldn't have, Roxy." And Roxy smiled and said, "I wanted to." And Mum looked even crosser and said, "But seriously you *shouldn't* have!"

7.2

Maths

The trick that Mum's friend Roxy played on us is this. She secretly bought pyjamas and toothbrushes when Mum and I were looking round the market. Then she invited us to stay overnight. Cool eh? And the trick I've been playing on you, Mr. Clark, is that Roxy is actually my step-grandmother!

On Sunday we were going to go out but Roxy wasn't feeling all that well so we stayed in and she taught me to play chess. We also played a game called Dobble. And lastly, we played darts. As Roxy said, darts teaches you maths better than a teacher can. (Sorry Mr. Clark!)

We got another postcard from Ari today. He's going back to America.

It felt good telling Mr. Clark that Roxy was my step-grandmother. It was a bit of a lie saying I'd been tricking him. Berry would have just told the truth in the first place, but I find that quite hard.

I felt sad at first that Roxy wasn't feeling well enough to go out. She said that some days she didn't have as much energy as others. Mum said it was amazing she had any energy at all at ninety one. I couldn't tell if that was Mum being impressed or being sulky. She was mainly sulky all weekend.

As it turned out we had a really good day. I didn't really get Chess but I loved the game called Dobble. The cards are round and are covered with little pictures of all sorts of things in all different sizes. You have to turn your cards over really quickly and spot the one thing on your card that's the same as something on the last card that was put down. Roxy beat me every time. Mum came last every time. Roxy said she only won because she'd been trained to have good powers of observation. I'm going to train myself to have good powers of observation.

Then she said we ought to play darts so I could get better at maths. We played four games. Mum won two of them (but it didn't make her any less sulky), I won one and Roxy won one. Roxy said she was no good at darts really and it was a fluke. She made me work out the scores every single time anyone had a turn. I'm really fast at adding up and taking away in my head now.

When we were driving home Mum said it was a mean trick that Roxy played on us, buying us jamas and stuff so it would be impossible for us to turn down the invitation to stay over. I said she was just being nice because she knew I wanted to stay. Then I asked if we could go back next weekend and Mum said, "No, definitely not. I want to spend some time with Rob." So then *I* was the sulky one. Mum asked me why I didn't like Rob and I said I didn't want him getting into our family, and Mum was quiet for ages then she said she didn't want Roxy getting into our family either. I said, "Yes but Roxy already *is* in our family, and Mum said, "No she's not. She's just the person who married my father."

We had a really long silence after that, before Mum said, "OK, let's make a deal. You can visit Roxy on your own next Saturday. I'll put you on the train and she can meet you at the other end. But in return you have to do something for me." "What?" I asked. "You have to come out for a nice meal with me and Rob so you can get to know each other better," she said. I shrugged and said, "Yeah OK," and Mum said, "I've not finished. You also have to join in the conversation and speak a bit more this time." I shrugged again and said, "OK," and made a plan to say more than fourteen words. But less than twenty.

Then I asked Mum if I could have violin lessons, her eyes went really wide like I'd asked if I could have bull fighting lessons and she said, "Where did that idea spring from?" And I said I liked the violin music that she kept listening to. And she looked sad again and said, "Nimrod?" I said I didn't know what it was called but it was by someone called Elgar, and Mum nodded and said, "Yes it's Nimrod from the Enigma Variations." And I let out a big gasp. *Enigma!* Now I *definitely* wanted to learn. "So can I, Mum?" I asked. And she said, "Ask me again when we get home. I need to work out if I can afford it."

7.3

After School Activities (2)

Dear Mr. Clark, I have changed my mind about after school activities. My mum wants me to learn violin, you see. She's going to phone you to ask how much it costs and where to get a violin from, but I thought I'd mention it too. Mum said it would be better if we didn't tell anyone about it, as she knows there are some people in the class who might tease me about learning violin. I hope that's OK.

Mr. Clark's not said a word to me about violin but Mum told me she talked to him on the phone and I'm starting lessons next week. My lesson will come after Berry's. I'm allowed to go on the computer while I'm waiting or I can read in the library. The lesson's going to last thirty minutes. Mum's going to hire a violin from a music shop until we find out that I definitely still like it even with all the practice I'll have to do. Mum told me I had to get it out of my head that learning the violin was something to be ashamed about. I think Mr. Clark might have told her about my Daily Status.

7.4

A Meal Out

*Last night we went out for a meal with one of Mum's
friends called Robyn. Robyn said SHe was paying. We
went to The Potted Shrimp. Have you ever been there
Mr. Clark? You might think from the name that it's a
fish restaurant but it's not. There's all sorts on the menu.
It was really popular though and we had to wait ages
and ages for our meal to be served. I had Calamari for
my starter, a steak burger for my main and one scoop of
pistachio and one scoop of vanilla ice cream for my
pudding. Rob was surprised I chose vanilla. (Rob is short
for Robyn by the way.) SHe thought I'd choose chocolate.*

*I liked the Calamari, but the steak burger was a bit
burnt and the bread was a bit dry. I had to chew hard
to get through it all. I mixed the ice cream up to melt it.
I don't like ice cream when it's freezing cold.*

So we were in this restaurant and we waited and waited for our
starters to arrive. Rob filled the time in by telling jokes. I don't think
he's the type to tell jokes really. He's too shy. Mum laughed like mad
but I kept a straight face. It wasn't easy because some of the jokes
were really funny. Then he suddenly called the waiter over and with
a cross expression on his face, said, "Excuse me, we've been waiting

fifty minutes." "It's just on its way, Sir," said the waiter. But it still took five minutes.

Then we had to wait more than half an hour after we'd finished the starter before the main course came. And when it did come Mum said she had to really chew and chew her meat before she could swallow it.

When it was time to pay the bill I wondered what Rob would say. Personally I didn't think the restaurant deserved any money for that meal. Rob must have agreed with me because he told the waiter we didn't enjoy the meal so he wouldn't be paying. I was quite surprised because Rob seemed too shy to say something like that. My heart was doing its thudding loudly thing. Mum looked a bit pink. The waiter looked like his eyebrows were going to shoot through the top of his head. "What about your wife?" he asked, smiling nervously at Mum. Then he turned to me. "And your son?"

I urgently tried to say, 'It's not his wife', but all I could say was "'s'not… s'not… s'not…" "See!" said Rob, without even blinking. "Joe thinks it tasted of snot! And I agree. Totally unacceptable I'm afraid, and not worth paying for." The waiter went to get the manager and the manager apologized like mad and said Rob only had to pay for the drinks. And guess what? He gave half the money he saved to me, and half to Mum. So I didn't mind so much when he held Mum's hand all the way home because I like him a bit better now. Not just because of the money. Because of the jokes – especially the one about the snot. And because he wasn't being all bright and energetic like he was with Noah and Olly that time. (My plan didn't work though. I spoke way more than 20 words.)

7.5

My Violin

Mum decided to get my violin from the music shop a day early to give me a nice surprise. She got a nice surprise herself too because when she was talking to the lady there, she found out that they're looking for someone to catalogue every single piece of music and every single instrument in the whole shop (and it's big!) And mum's got the job! She says she likes the idea of having a short-term job then changing to something else. She thinks she'll get a lot of experiences like that. She wants her next experience to be a gardening job.

My violin is a bit smaller than I thought it was going to be. Mum showed me how to tune it. We're not sure if we've done it right. Mum says the violin teacher will show me properly on Tuesday. When I first tried drawing the bow across the strings it bounced a bit and sounded all juddery. Then I pressed it too hard and it made a terrible noise but I kept trying for over two hours and now I've worked out how to play the first eleven notes of Mum's favourite piece of music, which is still Nimrod from the Enigma variations by Elgar. Mum thinks the violin teacher will be impressed.

Mum actually burst into tears when I showed her how I'd taught myself the first bit of Nimrod. She had Enigma Scruffball on her lap at the time and she buried her face in his fur and said, "I'm crying because I'm happy, Joe. You're so musical and I never knew. And you've specially chosen my favourite piece to learn first."

Later I heard Mum on the phone telling Rob about it. But I got a shock when I asked her what Rob thought about my violin skills because she said she'd been talking to Roxy not Rob. It was surprising because she was using the same soft laughing voice she uses for Rob. So I asked what Roxy thought, and Mum said Roxy was very pleased but not at all surprised because she'd known I'd be the type to be good at something like violin. I felt the rocket feeling when Mum said that.

8.1

A Big Surprise!

On Saturday I had the best day ever! My stepgranny, Roxy, took me to Bletchley Park. The actual place near Milton Keynes that was used as the top-secret intelligence decoding headquarters during the war. It was brilliant.

Roxy explained how all the thousands of people like the WRENS and the women from the WAAF, which stands for Women's Auxiliary Airforce, all over Britain, were listening in to the enemy's secret radio messages in special wireless intercept stations. They had to track the enemy radio network and write down every single letter or figure. Then they sent the messages to Bletchley Park to be decoded and also translated.

And guess what, Mr. Clark?

No, I'm going to keep you guessing till tomorrow!!!!!!!!

I couldn't believe it when Roxy said we were going to visit Bletchley Park. I told her it was my dream come true and she smiled a kind of secret smile to herself. She knew her way around Bletchley Park really well and she knew everything that was there and I asked her if she'd visited it before, and that's when she gave me the shock of my life. She said, "Joe, I worked here during the war. I was one of the WRENs who was posted here to decipher code."

I just stared at her in a daze and said, "Whoa! Cooooool!" And she smiled and said she'd tell me much more about codes next time she saw me. But I couldn't wait till then so I phoned up Mum and asked if Roxy could come back to our house and stay the night, and Mum sounded quite happy for once and said she could. Roxy bought a big note pad at the station, and on the train she explained loads about codes.

8.2

Ciphers

It's my violin lesson today after school. I can't wait.

But first here's some more interesting stuff about codes. Or you could call them CIPHERS. I like that word.

One cipher was invented by Julius Caesar. This is how it works. If you want to write NOAH, for example you look at the chart that I've written underneath and you'll see that N is actually Q when it's in the cipher because each letter of the alphabet has a code letter which is 3 letters further along in the alphabet.

A B C D E F G H I J K L M N O P Q R S T U V W X Y Z
D E F G H I J K L M N O P Q R S T U V W X Y Z A B C

See if you can work out these names, Mr. Clark:
R O O B   U R A B

With the Caesar code you can go along by any number up to 25! I'm going to write out all the 25 possible codes now. When you write it in a table like this it's called a Vigenère Square.

	A	B	C	D	E	F	G	H	I	J	K	L	M	N	O	P	Q	R	S	T	U	V	W	X	Y	Z
A	A	B	C	D	E	F	G	H	I	J	K	L	M	N	O	P	Q	R	S	T	U	V	W	X	Y	Z
B	B	C	D	E	F	G	H	I	J	K	L	M	N	O	P	Q	R	S	T	U	V	W	X	Y	Z	A
C	C	D	E	F	G	H	I	J	K	L	M	N	O	P	Q	R	S	T	U	V	W	X	Y	Z	A	B
D	D	E	F	G	H	I	J	K	L	M	N	O	P	Q	R	S	T	U	V	W	X	Y	Z	A	B	C
E	E	F	G	H	I	J	K	L	M	N	O	P	Q	R	S	T	U	V	W	X	Y	Z	A	B	C	D
F	F	G	H	I	J	K	L	M	N	O	P	Q	R	S	T	U	V	W	X	Y	Z	A	B	C	D	E
G	G	H	I	J	K	L	M	N	O	P	Q	R	S	T	U	V	W	X	Y	Z	A	B	C	D	E	F
H	H	I	J	K	L	M	N	O	P	Q	R	S	T	U	V	W	X	Y	Z	A	B	C	D	E	F	G
I	I	J	K	L	M	N	O	P	Q	R	S	T	U	V	W	X	Y	Z	A	B	C	D	E	F	G	H
J	J	K	L	M	N	O	P	Q	R	S	T	U	V	W	X	Y	Z	A	B	C	D	E	F	G	H	I
K	K	L	M	N	O	P	Q	R	S	T	U	V	W	X	Y	Z	A	B	C	D	E	F	G	H	I	J
L	L	M	N	O	P	Q	R	S	T	U	V	W	X	Y	Z	A	B	C	D	E	F	G	H	I	J	K
M	M	N	O	P	Q	R	S	T	U	V	W	X	Y	Z	A	B	C	D	E	F	G	H	I	J	K	L
N	N	O	P	Q	R	S	T	U	V	W	X	Y	Z	A	B	C	D	E	F	G	H	I	J	K	L	M
O	O	P	Q	R	S	T	U	V	W	X	Y	Z	A	B	C	D	E	F	G	H	I	J	K	L	M	N
P	P	Q	R	S	T	U	V	W	X	Y	Z	A	B	C	D	E	F	G	H	I	J	K	L	M	N	O
Q	Q	R	S	T	U	V	W	X	Y	Z	A	B	C	D	E	F	G	H	I	J	K	L	M	N	O	P
R	R	S	T	U	V	W	X	Y	Z	A	B	C	D	E	F	G	H	I	J	K	L	M	N	O	P	Q
S	S	T	U	V	W	X	Y	Z	A	B	C	D	E	F	G	H	I	J	K	L	M	N	O	P	Q	R
T	T	U	V	W	X	Y	Z	A	B	C	D	E	F	G	H	I	J	K	L	M	N	O	P	Q	R	S
U	U	V	W	X	Y	Z	A	B	C	D	E	F	G	H	I	J	K	L	M	N	O	P	Q	R	S	T
V	V	W	X	Y	Z	A	B	C	D	E	F	G	H	I	J	K	L	M	N	O	P	Q	R	S	T	U
W	W	X	Y	Z	A	B	C	D	E	F	G	H	I	J	K	L	M	N	O	P	Q	R	S	T	U	V
X	X	Y	Z	A	B	C	D	E	F	G	H	I	J	K	L	M	N	O	P	Q	R	S	T	U	V	W
Y	Y	Z	A	B	C	D	E	F	G	H	I	J	K	L	M	N	O	P	Q	R	S	T	U	V	W	X
Z	Z	A	B	C	D	E	F	G	H	I	J	K	L	M	N	O	P	Q	R	S	T	U	V	W	X	Y

That took me ages, Mr. Clark! But there are even more complicated codes. And in case you're wondering how I know about this, Mr. Clark, I got it all from Roxy, my granny, because, guess what, she used to be one of the top secret workers at BLETCHLEY PARK! (Bet you couldn't have guessed that!)

I like calling my step-granny Granny Roxy and I think Berry would have thought that was nice and honest of me. Also, it was really cool learning all the different ways you could decode code. Granny Roxy and I are going to write all our text messages in code from now on! But I'm going to be able to see her more soon because she's moving to London. She says she wants to be nearer to us and anyway her house in Norwich is miles too big. She's buying a flat with one spare room.

When we got back to my house on Saturday, the sun was still shining and Mum was out on the patio at the back drinking tea with Rob and two other people who turned out to be Rob's mum and dad. They're way younger than Roxy.

Rob and Roxy shook hands and I told everyone about Bletchley Park and Granny Roxy being one of the secret workers there. Mum and Roxy exchanged a look and I asked Mum if she knew already. She nodded and gave Roxy a smile. Then she really surprised me because she gave her a tight hug and said, "Thank you for having Joe today. I'm really grateful." And Roxy smiled and said, "Any time." I'm pleased that Mum and Roxy get along now.

8.3

My First Violin Lesson

My violin lesson was brilliant. This is my teacher's name in Caesar code. Here's a clue: the letter that appears most in the code is actually S in my teacher's name. So now you've got to work out how many letters along in the alphabet I've done the code. You'll have to look at that Vigenere Square I did!

SOYY YEQKY

I can already play a scale and some more of Nimrod plus some of Supercalifragilisticexpialidocious. (I wouldn't like to write that in code!)

The only bad thing about my lesson happened just before I went in, when Berry came out. I'd planned to give her a big smile and ask if we could be friends again but I didn't get the chance because she said to me, "So you're finally being honest with yourself and doing what *you* want to do, Joe, and not letting creeps like Croppo control you? Good." I didn't know what to say after that and anyway it was too late because she was walking away, but before she went round the corner I quickly blurted out, "I've taught myself to play some of Enigma Variations." She stopped in her tracks, turned round slowly and looked at me properly. "I love that music," she said quietly. Then she walked off again.

8.4

The Author Visit

An author came into school yesterday. It was really interesting. I liked it when some people read out loud from their Daily Status entries. I read out everything about Bletchley Park. The author thought it was really interesting and asked me how I knew it all and when I said about Granny Roxy, she was even more interested and wanted to know all about her. Everyone was silent while I was talking. Croppo had written about someone in a motorbike accident. It was quite sad. Berry had written something about a boy shoplifting. The author asked her if it was true and she said yes, but, personally, I think she made it up.

After the Daily Status reading in the classroom, the whole school had to go into the hall for a kind of assembly with the author. She asked if anyone wanted to volunteer to come up to the front. I shot my hand up then looked round expecting to see loads of hands. Mine was the only one and I wondered if I'd missed something. It wouldn't be surprising. I hadn't been listening properly. My head was full of Berry's story. I'd decided to tell her the truth about what happened at Debenhams straight after assembly.

I wasn't worried about being chosen as a volunteer. I guessed

the author wanted me to do something about imagination. Or
words. She already knew I was good at being imaginative but she
didn't know I was extra good at words since I've known Roxy.

So I went to the front and she said, "Remind me of your
name?" I said, "Joe." She said, "Well Joe, which dance are you going
to show us?" I thought I was going to fall over with shock. This was
terrible. I couldn't dance. I should have listened properly then I'd
never have been in this mess.

Lots of people sniggered. The teachers looked alarmed. I was
about to mumble something about changing my mind when I
caught sight of Berry and saw the look she was giving me. She was
sitting up straight and leaning forwards. And she was wearing her
magnet eyes of steel. They were flashing a message at me just like
before. The message said *Go on, You can do this*. And then she
blinked and the message was stronger. This time I was going to be

honest with myself and do it for Berry because I wanted to. Before I knew it, I'd said, "Irish."

I looked down and concentrated until I got a picture in my head of Riverdance. It felt like I could hear the music and everything. Then I looked back up again and kind of sprang into the air. I kept my arms rigid by my side just like the Riverdance people did and I tapped my shoes hard and fast and picked my knees up high and really felt like I actually was one of those people on the stage. If there'd been real music I could have done it even better. I forgot completely where I was and just carried on and on for about ten minutes. Well it was probably only one minute but it felt like a long time. Then I stopped.

That was when I realized I was in the school hall, not on a stage in the lead role of a hit show. I closed my eyes kind of hoping that when I opened them again I'd find it was all a dream.

But then it hit me that everyone was clapping. And Berry was standing up, clapping over her head and nodding so you could hardly tell, and giving me her best best look. There was no steel in her eyes this time. Only a sparkle look. Then the teachers stood up too, and so did every single person in the whole hall. Including Croppo. And the clapping got louder with whistling and cheering. And the author had to really shout so I could hear her above the noise. "That was the most brilliant thing I've ever experienced on a school visit, Joe. You're an inspiration and I shall definitely be writing about you on my website!" And as I went back to my place, lots of people patted me on the back. Croppo looked like he'd swallowed a fly. I looked across at Berry. She still had her sparkle eyes and I kind of knew I'd never again see that steely look or the maggot look or the poo on the shoe look. I'd passed the Berry test. It was the best feeling in the world.

8.5

My Last Daily Status

I'm quite sad that this is the last ever status. I'll try to write everything I want to write.

I live with my Mum and my brilliant stepdad, Rob. Mum and Rob aren't married yet but they're going to be soon. Rob's last name is Mitchel and Mum says that when they're married she's going to be called Annie Mitchel-Barnes and I'm getting my name changed too. I'm going to be called Joe Mitchel-Barnes! Yay! It's like I've got a middle name! And my family's grown even more than that because of Granny Rox (which you can also write Granny rocks!) PLUS I've also got a step-grandmother and a step-grandfather who are Rob's parents.

Granny Rox has had an offer on her house in Norwich and she's not moving to London after all. She's moving near us. We're giving her this little dog we've got called Cashew because Mum's got fed up with all the guffing it does. I pretended it was our neighbour's dog, Mr Clark, because I was embarrassed, but I'm not any more. Granny Rox doesn't care if people think it's her guffing. She's calling the dog Scruffball, which was what I've always called it. Rob and Mum want to get a – wait for it - Great Dane!

Ari has Skyped me from America. I didn't used to know anyone outside England, but I do now!

Rob's given me an early birthday present. It's a brand new violin. It's the best present ever and now Mum doesn't have to pay for the hired violin any more. Rob knows how to play the piano. He's got a keyboard. He says he'll accompany me when I'm practising.

We've abandoned the Code Club because we keep forgetting to have meetings.

Dora's nursery told Olly's mum and dad that Dora is gifted. Olly's dad asked them if that was the same as having the gift of the gab.

Y   esterday it was our play. I did sing the solo in Rumpelstiltskin in the end. Berry said I rocked. Rob said I was the best thing in the whole play. But he's biased. Lots of people patted me on the back and said, "You were awesome, Joe!" Croppo said, "Well done, Joe." When we walked home there was a rainbow in the sky.

Granny Rox and I talk about lots of things. I told her praying doesn't work because of the time I prayed for an owner to turn up for Scruffball. She said praying does work because an owner did turn up. Her! She also said that she'd said a prayer every day for fifteen years that Mum would get in touch with her, and then Mum did. On Thursdays next term it's going to be Mini Orchestra. I'll get to sit next to the girl I like best in our whole class. This girl and I talk a lot. Girls talk about things that boys don't usually like talking about much, for example we both laughed at ourselves for getting the wrong end of the stick. I got the wrong end of the stick thinking that my mum had been shoplifting when she hadn't, and this girl got the wrong end of the stick thinking I was shoplifting when all I was doing was putting everything back.

If you want to know who this girl is, you'll have to break the code, Mr. Clark. (Here's your clue: Think of a word that goes after straw to make another word. Then use that word instead of 'straw'. Next think of a word that goes after gold to make another word, and use that word instead of 'gold.' You can keep the TO just as it is.)

Straw TO Gold

The End

Instructions To The Code Breaker
(in code, of course!)

CLUE: Follow the pattern I've started off for you! When you come to the end, go back to the beginning and continue the pattern. You'll have to put your own full stops in!)

If you manage *publisher your name* to crack this *and address you* code why not *can write by* write in to snail mail or the publisher find email as a out who the bonus you will publisher is by get an extra looking at the surprise gift if flyleaf at the you manage to beginning of the work out the book you will name of my automatically win a best friend which bookmark signed by appears in code me all you somewhere in the *have to do* book good luck *is tell the* from me, Joe!

Here are the answers to the other codes from the book:

1.2	Carrot top
1.3	Code breaking is fun
1.4	Diamond Cottage
2.1	48 hours
2.4	Alsatian
2.4	Beagle
2.4	Great Dane
2.4	Bulldog
2.4	Boxer
3.2	Rumpelstiltskin
4.2	Rob
5.3	What you are looking into right now
5.4	Riverdance
6.5	Scooter
8.2	Olly Roxy
8.3	Miss Sykes
8.5	Berry T O Smith